Anonymous

Act of Incorporation and Bye-Laws

Anatiposi

Anonymous

Act of Incorporation and Bye-Laws

Reprint of the original.

1st Edition 2023 | ISBN: 978-3-38230-062-3

Anatiposi Verlag is an imprint of Outlook Verlagsgesellschaft mbH.

Verlag (Publisher): Outlook Verlag GmbH, Zeilweg 44, 60439 Frankfurt, Deutschland
Vertretungsberechtigt (Authorized to represent): E. Roepke, Zeilweg 44, 60439 Frankfurt, Deutschland
Druck (Print): Books on Demand GmbH, In de Tarpen 42, 22848 Norderstedt, Deutschland

ACT OF INCORPORATION

AND

BYE-LAWS

RURAL CEMETERY COMPANY.

ESTABLISHED 1848.

SAINT JOHN, N. B.

PRINTED BY W. L. AVERY, PRINCE WILLIAM STREET.

SAINT JOHN RURAL CEMETERY.

SEVERAL Gentlemen having become impressed
with the idea, that from the rapid increase of the City of
Saint John, other and more extensive burying accom-
modations should be procured than the unsightly and
confined spots, which have hitherto been in use,
but unwilling at the same time to take upon themselves
the selection of a site or other initiatory measures
connected with the undertaking, they thought it the
most proper method to request by Circular, that each
Denomination of Christians in the City of Saint John
and Parish of Portland, should unite in appointing a
Committee to act with the projectors, in arranging the
matter.

The following Prospectus was printed, and sent
with a Circular to the different Office-bearers of Con-
gregations therein mentioned. This took place in the
months of April and May, Eighteen Hundred and
Forty Seven.

PROSPECTUS

*Of a Joint Stock Company to be formed in the City of Saint John,
for the purpose of purchasing a Piece of Ground, say from
Fifty to One Hundred Acres, in the neighbourhood of the City,
and forming the same into a Rural Cemetery,* OPEN EQUALLY
to all.

THE necessity existing for a Public Cemetery
for this large and growing City is painfully but strongly
borne in upon the minds of the projectors of the present Company when viewing the crowded condition of
the Cemeteries now in use; and an appeal is now

made to all Denominations to join in procuring a Cemetery, which from its contemplated extent, will not
for a long series of years be open to the objections
now existing.

It is proposed to raise the sum of Two Thousand
Five Hundred Pounds, in a Thousand Shares of Two
Pounds Ten Shillings each.

It being the object of the projectors to interest in
their scheme all classes and denominations in the City
and the Parishes adjoining, it is proposed to allot, at
the outset, Fifty Shares to each Congregation, and One
Hundred Shares to the City Authorities, viz. :

ROMAN CATHOLICS,	2 Congregations,	100
EPISCOPALIANS,	4	"	200
PRESBYTERIANS,	4	"	200
BAPTISTS,	4	"	200
METHODISTS,	3	"	150
CONGREGATIONALISTS,	1	"	50
THE CORPORATION,			100
			1000

—which number of Shares, if not subscribed for
within ———— days from the opening of the Subscription Book, will then be open to any persons who may
wish to subscribe—deprecating always the idea of their
being taken on speculation.

It is also proposed that the Ground shall be laid
out and ornamented after the plan of similar institu-
tions in other countries, so far as the nature of the
ground will admit, reserving space for the erection of
a small Chapel, and a Keeper and Gardener's resi-
dences ; and that the produce of the sale of Lots,
under the management of the Directors of the Company, shall be appropriated, say, One-half towards
paying the expenses of laying out, keeping in order,
and ornamenting the Grounds, and the other half to

refund to the Stockholders their original outlay with interest, until they shall be paid in full, and after their being so paid in full, then One-quarter of the nett proceeds in perpetuity to them as a bonus on their shares.

Also: That Twenty Five per centum of the sum subscribed for by any party shall be paid in cash at the time of subscribing, and that the remaining Seventy Five per centum be called in as it may be required, the same to be at the discretion of the Directors : that so soon as the Stock shall be all taken up, a Meeting of the Shareholders shall be called for the purpose of framing Bye Laws for the regulation of the affairs of the Company, and electing so many of the Shareholders to serve as Directors as may be agreed on at the said General Meeting.

—

Replies to the Circular were received from the Church of England, appointing Dr. BOTSFORD and Mr. JOSEPH FAIRWEATHER ; from Saint Andrew's Church, appointing Mr. ADAM JACK ; from Saint Stephen's Church, appointing Mr. JOHN BRYDEN ; from the Independent Church, appointing Mr. W. G. LAWTON ; from the Free Presbyterian Church, appointing Mr. W. PARKS ; from the Covenanters, appointing Mr. JAMES AGNEW ; and from the Baptist Church, appointing Mr. SOLOMON HERSEY and Mr. A. McL. SEELY. The Roman Catholics and Methodists did not reply to the Circular.

The Committee after a lengthened and labored investigation of all the localities in the vicinity of Saint John, likely to be suitable, concluded on purchasing Seventy Acres of Land from JAMES PETERS, Junior, Esquire, and Forty Acres adjoining, from HENRY GILBERT, Esquire, situate on the Marsh Road, about One and a Quarter miles from the City, and possessing advantages for the contemplated purpose, far exceeding those of any other site examined. The price of the first was Two Thousand Pounds, and the last, Six Hundred Pounds ; in both cases a reserve being made of a suitable Burying Lot for each proprietor.

Mr. JAMES PETERS, Junior, died shortly after his offer was accepted, but his devisees, Dr. GEORGE P. PETERS and Mr. EDWARD B. PETERS, consented to complete the sale.

The following was the heading of the Subscription List handed round :

RURAL CEMETERY,

Capital £3000, in Twelve Hundred Shares of £2 10s. each.

THE Projectors of the Rural Cemetery, with the Delegates appointed by the different Denominations, having selected and secured, for the sum of Two Thousand Six Hundred Pounds, One Hundred and Ten Acres of Land, within One and a Quarter miles of the City, known as the Property which belonged to the late JAMES PETERS, Junior, Esquire, and to HENRY GILBERT, Esquire, and which they consider well adapted to the purpose contemplated, have now to offer the Stock to the Public.

They intend to offer it, in the first instance, to the Denominations engaged in the undertaking, in equal proportions, so that all parties may have an equal control in the management of the Cemetery.

Any portion of the Stock not taken up within *One Month* from this date, will be offered to the Public generally.

The whole of the Capital will be called for, and the purchase money paid in full.

The Committee intend, in the meantime, to offer a Premium for the best Plan for laying out the Ground, which Plan shall be submitted before the Stock is called in.

The following are the conditions on which the Stock shall be taken, and which shall be held as the *Constitution* of the Company:—

1st. That the whole Grounds, with all Buildings to be erected (with the exception of a portion of ground to be selected by the Committee, and laid aside for the Church of England), shall be forever free to all Denominations.

2d. That so soon as the Stock is paid, the choice of Lots shall be offered at Auction, at such upset price as the Directors shall think fit.

3d. That One-half of the purchase money of the Lots shall be used for ornamenting the Grounds, the other Half to be paid to the Stockholders until they be paid in full, with interest at Eight per centum per annum, after which the whole proceeds shall be laid out on the Grounds.

4th. That the Stockholders shall, in the first instance, elect Twelve Directors from amongst themselves, each Share to have a vote but that each Proprietor of a Lot shall afterwards have a vote and be eligible as a Director,—until the whole Stock with interest is paid, when the Proprietors of Lots shall form the Company. The Directors to be elected Annually.

5th. That the Directors shall not be at liberty to depart from the Plan of the Grounds adopted, unless the intended alteration be approved of by Three-fourths of their number.

LeBARON BOTSFORD, M. D.,
R. JARDINE, *Secretary.*   *Chairman.*
Saint John, August 13, 1847.

———

The Committee offered a Premium of Thirty Pounds for the best, and Ten Pounds for the second best Plan for laying out the Grounds. There were only two competitors, Mr. M. STEAD and Mr. G. N. SMITH, and the Premiums were awarded to these Gentlemen in the order in which they stand.

The Committee also selected a portion of the Ground for the Church of England.

The following is a List of the Original Shareholders:

Honorable Chief Justice Chipman,
    "   Hugh Johnston,
    "   R. L. Hazen,
    "   John Robertson,

James Kirk,
Thomas Pettingell,
John Duncan,
Robert Jardine,
John Wishart,
William J. Ritchie,
William Parks,
Thomas Parks,
William Hawkes,
John Hawkes,
John Hammond,
George P. Peters,
Edward B. Peters,
William G. Lawton,
H. Bowyer Smith,
Benjamin Smith,
John Pollok,
Thomas Davidson,
Henry Chubb,
George Young,
William Wright,
James Pettingell,

Joseph Fairweather,
R. Richey,
J. A. Morrison,
Samuel Neil,
R. F. Hazen,
J. V. Thurgar,
Samuel Spiller,
A. McL. Seeley,
Solomon Hersey,
Samuel Robinson,
William Jack,
Adam Jack,
Charles C. Stewart,
Charles Johnston,
Isaac L. Bedell,
Frederick A. Wiggins,
John H. Gray,
Thomas Gilchrist,
John M. Robinson,
James Dunn,
James Reed,
Beverley Robinson,

Dr. LeB. Botsford,
John Bryden,
Charles Drury,
John M. Walker,
W. R. M. Burtis,
Duncan Robertson,
George Wheeler,
R. W. Crookshank, Jr.
Alexander Gilchrist,
John M'Lardy,
George L. Lovett,
Matthew Stead,
A. C. O. Trentowsky,
Edward Sancton,
James Hancock,
Francis Drake,
B. C. Chaloner,

Zebulon Ring,
Thomas M'Henry,
J. W. M. Irish,
Captain Moran,
Peter Drake,
Valentine Harding,
Charles Hay,
George W. Gorham,
James Brayley,
S. B. Estey,
John T. Smith,
E. H. Duval,
J. H. Read,
Manuel Francis,
A. W. Lawrence,
William Hayward,
R. & A. Grier.

The Stock having been taken up, a Meeting of the Stockholders was called by Public Advertisement for the Thirteenth of December, Eighteen Hundred and Forty Seven, at which time Twelve Directors were chosen to manage the affairs of the Company; and they were further requested to prepare a Bill for the Incorporation of the Company; which was afterwards passed into a Law, and is as follows.

AN ACT

FOR THE INCORPORATION OF THE SAINT JOHN RURAL CEMETERY COMPANY.

Passed 30th March, A. D. 1848.

WHEREAS from the great increase of the Population of the City and County of Saint John, the want of a suitable place for the Burial of the Dead is much required.

I. *Be it therefore enacted by the Lieutenant Governor, Legislative Council and Assembly,* That

ROBERT JARDINE, Honorable ROBERT L. HAZEN, BE-
VERLEY ROBINSON, JAMES PETTINGELL, SOLOMON
HERSEY, WILLIAM G. LAWTON, GEORGE P. PETERS,
JOHN M. WALKER, WILLIAM PARKS, CHARLES DRURY,
ADAM JACK, and LE BARON BOTSFORD, their Associates,
Successors, and Assigns, be and they are hereby de-
clared to be a body Politic and Corporate, by the
name of *The Corporation of the Saint John Rural
Cemetery Company*, and by that name shall have all
the general powers and privileges made incident to a
Corporation by Act of Assembly of this Province.

II. *And be it enacted,* That the Capital Stock
of the said Corporation shall consist of the sum
of Three Thousand Pounds, and shall be divided into
Twelve Hundred Shares of Two Pounds Ten Shillings
each, and be paid in such sums, and at such time or
times, as the Directors of the said Corporation shall
from time to time appoint. And every Shareholder
in the said Corporation shall have and be entitled to
have a Certificate under the Seal of the said Corporation, and signed by the President and Secretary
thereof, certifying his Property in such Shares as shall
be expressed in the Certificate.

III. *And be it enacted,* That whenever any
Assessment shall be made, it shall be the duty of
the Treasurer to give notice thereof in two or more
newspapers printed in the said City of Saint John,
requiring payment of the same within Thirty days,
and if any Shareholder shall neglect or refuse to pay
to the Treasurer, the amount of such assessment upon
his Share or Shares, at the time prescribed, it shall be
the duty of the Treasurer to advertize such delinquent's
Share or Shares for sale at Public Auction, giving at
least Ten days notice of the time and place of such
sale ; and such Share or Shares upon which the Assessment or Assessments, or Instalments thereof shall

then remain unpaid, shall be sold to the highest bidder, and such sale shall be a legal transfer of the Share or Shares so sold to the purchaser or purchasers thereof, and shall be recorded accordingly in the Book so to be kept by the Directors for that purpose as aforesaid; and such purchaser or purchasers shall be entitled to receive a Certificate in the form prescribed in the Second Section of this Act.

IV. And whereas a Piece of Land containing One Hundred and Ten Acres, and lately belonging to the late JAMES PETERS, Junior, and HENRY GILBERT, Esquires, situate in the Parish of Simonds, in the County of Saint John, has been secured for the purpose of a Burying Ground, and with the exception of a portion which has been laid aside for the Church of England, shall be forever free to all denominations of Christians, to be divided into Lots and sold to such individuals as may be willing to purchase the same, and which said Land is described as follows, to-wit: Beginning on the North Eastern side of the Marsh Road at the North West corner of Lands owned by THOMAS TRAFTON, thence North Forty Seven degrees Thirty minutes West along the Marsh Road Twenty chains Ninety One links, to the South Western line of WIGGINS' Marsh; thence South Forty degrees East to edge of Upland; thence along the edge of Upland and Marsh to the South West line of JARVIS' Upland; thence South Forty degrees East Twenty Three chains to the Old Westmorland Road; thence along the Old Westmorland Road Thirty Seven chains South Westerly to the North Eastern line of THOMAS TRAFTON's Farm; thence North Forty degrees West Twenty Seven chains and Fifty links to the place of beginning: *Be it therefore enacted*, That the said Land above described be, and hereby is declared to be exempted from all Rates, Assessments and Taxes, so long as the same shall remain dedicated to the purposes of a Cemetery.

V. *And be it enacted,* That all persons who shall hereafter become Proprietors of Lots in the Cemetery aforesaid, of a size not less each than One Hundred and Fifty Square Feet, shall thereby become Members of the said Corporation, and shall have, and be entitled to have a Certificate under the Seal of the Corporation, signed by the Secretary, in the form following :

SAINT JOHN RURAL CEMETERY COMPANY.

No.

This is to Certify, that A. B. is the Proprietor of Lot No. containing sqare feet, on *(Avenue or Path)* in the Saint John Rural Cemetery, situate in the Parish of Simonds in the County of Saint John, subject to the Rules, Regulations, and Bye Laws of the said Corporation, and for which he has this day paid the sum of

In testimony whereof the Seal of the said Corporation is hereunto affixed, the day of A. D. 184

C. D.,

(L. S.) Secretary.

And such Certificate shall constitute a valid instrument of transfer of such Lot or Lots as may be expressed therein, and shall be held by the purchaser or purchasers thereof for the use of Burial only, subject nevertheless to all the Bye Laws of the said Corporation.

VI. *And be it enacted,* That a General Meeting of the Stockholders and Proprietors of the said Corporation shall be held at the City of Saint John on the First Monday in May in each and every year, for the purpose of choosing Twelve Directors for the management of the said Corporation, which Directors so chosen shall remain in office for One Year, or until others are chosen in their stead. And shall at their First Meeting after the Election choose one of their number President of the said Corporation : Provided always that not less than Five Directors do form a Quorum for the transaction of business ; and in case of the absence of the President, the Directors shall have power to appoint one of their number Chairman for the occasion.

VII. *And be it enacted,* That the Directors for the time being, shall and may appoint a Secretary and Treasurer, and such other Officers, Clerks, and Servants as they or the major part of them shall think necessary for executing the business of the said Corporation, and shall allow them (out of the Funds of the said Corporation) such compensation for their respective services as to them shall appear reasonable and proper. And the Directors shall likewise exercise such other powers and authorities for the well regulating the affairs and managing the business of the said Corporation as shall be prescribed by the Bye Laws.

VIII. *And be it enacted,* That every person owning a Share in the Capital Stock of the said Corporation, and every proprietor of a Lot of not less, each, than One Hundred and Fifty Square Feet, shall be a Member of the said Corporation and entitled to vote at all Meetings of the said Corporation ; and Members may give as many votes as they may own Shares, and absent Members may vote by proxy, such proxy being a Shareholder, and producing sufficient authority in writing from his Constituent. Provided nevertheless that no Stockholder by himself or proxies shall have more than One Hundred votes.

IX. *And be it enacted,* That the Shares of the said Corporation shall be assignable and transferable according to such Rules and Regulations as may be established in that behalf, but no assignment or trans-

fer shall be valid and effectual unless the same shall
be entered and registered in a Book to be kept by the
Directors for that purpose.

X. *And be it enacted*, That in case of any vacancy among the Directors by death, resignation or
disqualification or otherwise, then and in either of
such cases the said Directors shall and may fill up
such vacancy by choosing one of the Shareholders or
Proprietors of Lots of not less, each, than One Hundred and Fifty Square Feet. And the person so
chosen by the Directors shall serve until another is
chosen in his room.

XI. *And be it enacted*, That the several Shareholders in the said Corporation shall be Members of
the same until they shall be repaid, out of the Funds
of the said Corporation, the amounts by them respectively invested, together with interest on the same at
the rate of Eight per centum per annum, when they
shall cease to have any interest in the said Cemetery,
and the property shall from thence be vested in ROBERT
JARDINE, HENRY GILBERT, JOHN M. WALKER, GEORGE
P. PETERS, JAMES PETTINGELL, WILLIAM G. LAWTON,
LeBARON BOTSFORD, WILLIAM PARKS, and EDWARD
B. PETERS, being the present Proprietors of Lots in the
said Cemetery, and all future Proprietors of Lots of
not less, each, than One Hundred and Fifty Square
Feet.

XII. *And be it enacted*, That from and after the
payment to the several Shareholders of the amount
so invested by them respectively, together with interest
as in and by the Eleventh Section is provided, the
proceeds of all sales of Lots after deducting the annual expenses of the said Cemetery, shall be forever
devoted and applied to the preservation, improvement,
embellishment, and enlargement of the said Cemetery,
and for no other purpose whatsoever.

XIII. *And be it enacted*, That if any person or per-
ons shall wilfully destroy, mutilate, injure, or remove
ny Tomb, Monument, Grave Stone, or other struc-
ure placed in the Cemetery aforesaid, or any Fence,
Railing, or other work for the protection or ornament
or any Tomb, Monument, Grave Stone, or other struc-
ure aforesaid, or shall wilfully destroy, remove, cut,
break or injure any Tree, Shrub or Plant within the
imits of the said Cemetery, or shall play at any game
or sport, or discharge any gun or other firearm, save
at a Military Funeral, within the said Cemetery, or who
shall wilfully and unlawfully disturb any persons as-
sembled in the Cemetery for the purpose of burying any
body therein, or who shall commit any nuisance within
the said Cemetery, shall be deemed guilty of a misde-
meanor, and shall upon conviction thereof before any
Justice of the Peace, be punished by a fine of not less
than One Pound, nor more than Five Pounds, or be
committed to the Common Gaol for the space of not
more than Ten days, according to the nature and aggra-
vation of the offence. And such offender shall also be
liable in an action of trespass to be brought against him
in any Court of competent jurisdiction in the name of
the Corporation of the Saint John Rural Cemetery Company, to pay all such damages as shall have been
occasioned by his or their unlawful act or acts, which
money when recovered shall be applied by the said
Corporation to the reparation of the Property de-
stroyed or injured as above. And members of the
said Corporation shall be competent witnesses in such
suit.

XIV. *And be it enacted*, That the Lots in the
said Cemetery shall not be levied upon or taken in
Execution, but shall be altogether free from seizure
at the suit of any person or persons whomsoever, and
that the Property in any of such Burial Lots or part

thereof, shall not prevent any confined debtor from receiving support under the Law in force for the relief and support of confined debtors.

———

OFFICERS OF THE CORPORATION,
For 1848.

—

ROBERT JARDINE, President.

DIRECTORS.

DR. PETERS,	HON. R. L. HAZEN,
DR. BOTSFORD,	ROBERT JARDINE,
CHARLES DRURY,	WILLIAM PARKS,
BEVERLEY ROBINSON.	WILLIAM G. LAWTON,
SOLOMON HERSEY,	JOHN M. WALKER,
JAMES PETTINGELL,	ADAM JACK.

EDWARD B. PETERS, Secretary and Treasurer.

M. STEAD, Landscape Gardener.

ROBERT MILLS, Superintendent.

OFFICERS OF THE CORPORATION.

1852.

DR. BOTSFORD, President.

DR. BOTSFORD,
DR. PETERS,
C. DRURY,
B. ROBINSON,
J. PETTINGELL,
J. M. WALKER,

W. PARKS,
W. G. LAWTON,
W. J. RITCHIE,
S. HERSEY,
W. JACK,
W. WRIGHT.

EDWARD B. PETERS, Secretary and Treasurer.

ROBERT MILLS, Superintendent.

1853.

DR. BOTSFORD, President.

DR. BOTSFORD,
DR. PETERS,
C. DRURY,
B. ROBINSON,
J. PETTINGELL,
J. M. WALKER,

W. PARKS,
W. G. LAWTON,
W. J. RITCHIE,
S. HERSEY,
W. JACK,
W. WRIGHT.

EDWARD B. PETERS, Secretary and Treasurer.

ROBERT MILLS, Superintendent.

1854.

DR. BOTSFORD, President.

DR. BOTSFORD,
DR. PETERS,
C. DRURY,
B. ROBINSON,
J. PETTINGELL,
J. M. WALKER,

W. PARKS,
W. G. LAWTON,
W. J. RITCHIE,
S. HERSEY,
W. JACK,
W. WRIGHT.

EDWARD B. PETERS, Secretary and Treasurer.

ROBERT MILLS, Superintendent.

OFFICERS OF THE CORPORATION.

1855.

DR. BOTSFORD, President.

DR. BOTSFORD,	W. PARKS,
DR. PETERS,	S. HERSEY,
C. DRURY,	W. J. RITCHIE,
J. M. WALKER,	W. G. LAWTON,
B. ROBINSON,	W. WRIGHT,
J. PETTINGELL,	W. JACK.

EDWARD B. PETERS, Secretary and Treasurer.

JOHN ADAMS, Superintendent.

1856.

DR. BOTSFORD, President.

DR. BOTSFORD,	B. ROBINSON,
DR. PETERS,	W. G. LAWTON,
J. PETTINGELL,	S. HERSEY,
W. PARKS,	W. J. RITCHIE,
C. DRURY,	W. WRIGHT,
J. M. WALKER,	W. JACK.

EDWARD B. PETERS, Secretary and Treasurer.

JOHN ADAMS, Superintendent.

1857.

DR. BOTSFORD, President.

DR. BOTSFORD,	W. PARKS,
DR. PETERS,	C. DRURY,
J. PETTINGELL,	J. M. WALKER,
B. ROBINSON,	S. HERSEY,
W. G. LAWTON,	W. JACK,
W. J. RITCHIE,	W. WRIGHT.

EDWARD B. PETERS, Secretary and Treasurer.

JOHN ADAMS, Superintendent.

OFFICERS OF THE CORPORATION.

1858.

J. M. WALKER, President.

DR. BOTSFORD,
C. DRURY,
J. PETTINGELL,
S. HERSEY,
J. M. WALKER,
W. WRIGHT,

HON. W. J. RITCHIE,
W. JACK,
B. ROBINSON,
W. PARKS,
W. G. LAWTON,
C. C. STEWART.

EDWARD B. PETERS, Secretary and Treasurer.

JOHN ADAMS, Superintendent.

1859.

J. M. WALKER, President.

DR. BOTSFORD,
C. DRURY,
J. PETTINGELL,
J. M. WALKER,
W. WRIGHT,
W. JACK,

HON. W. J. RITCHIE,
W. PARKS,
W. G. LAWTON,
HON. A. McL. SEELY,
R. JARDINE,
G. SIDNEY SMITH.

EDWARD B. PETERS, Secretary and Treasurer.

JOHN ADAMS, Superintendent.

AN ACT

TO AMEND AN ACT FOR THE INCORPORATION OF THE SAINT JOHN CEMETERY COMPANY.

Passed 3d May, 1853.

WHEREAS the time for holding the annual general meeting of the Saint John Rural Cemetery Company is found very inconvenient, and it has become necessary that the same should be altered ;—

Be it therefore enacted, &c.—1. So much of the sixth Section of the Act of incorporation as applies to the holding of the annual general meeting of the said Company is hereby repealed ; and in lieu thereof, from and after this present year, the annual general meeting of the stockholders and proprietors of the said Company shall be held on the first Monday in April in each and every year, for the purpose of choosing Directors, &c., as expressed in an by the said sixth Section.

2. The lots in the said Cemetery shall be indivisible, but upon the death of any proprietor of any lot in the said Cemetery containing not less than one hundred and fifty square feet, the devisee of such lot, or the heir at law, as the case may be, shall be entitled to all the privileges of membership, and if there be more than one devisee or heir at law of such lot, the Directors for the time being shall designate which of the said devisees or heirs at law shall represent the said lot and vote in the meetings of the Corporation, but nothing herein contained shall prevent the heirs at law of such proprietor of a lot from burying in the same lot under the bye laws of the said Company.

BYE-LAWS

OF THE

SAINT JOHN

RURAL CEMETERY COMPANY.

—◦✦◦—

AT a Meeting of the Shareholders of *The Saint John Rural Cemetery Company*, on the first day of May, in the year of our Lord one thousand eight hundred and forty eight, the following Bye-Laws were adopted.

Cemetery.

1. The present upset price of Lots of One Hundred and Fifty Square Feet, or Fifteen by Ten Feet, shall be Five Pounds; and in proportion for more or less.

2. A choice of Lots shall be offered at Auction from time to time, but private sales may be made of Lots when required for actual use, at such prices as the Directors may fix.

3. A portion of Ground shall be laid aside for the Poor, in which bodies may be deposited at Five Shillings each.

4. A portion of Ground shall be laid aside for Public use, in which bodies may be deposited at Ten Shillings each.

18

5. A portion of Ground has been selected, which the Church of England has a right to consecrate, and within which, if required, interments must be made subject to the Rules of that Denomination.

6. The Servants of the Cemetery shall dig Graves at the following rates :—Ten Shillings from the first November to the first of May ; Five Shillings from first of May to the first of November ; if they have to cut through rock, the actual expenses of cutting will be charged.

Proprietors,

1. The Proprietor of a Lot of One Hundred and Fifty Square Feet or upwards shall have a right to enclose the same with a Wall or Fence, the form to be approved of by the Superintendent ; also to build Vaults, erect Monuments ; and cultivate Plants and Shrubs within the same.

2. If any Trees or Shrubs shall be deemed by the Superintendent detrimental to the Grounds, he shall, upon order from the Board, have right to enter upon such Lots and remove such Trees or Shrubs, or such parts thereof as he may deem detrimental.

3. If any Monument, Structure or Inscription be placed in or upon any Lot, which shall be determined by the Directors to be offensive or improper, the Directors shall have a right to enter upon such Lot and remove such offensive or improper object ; provided that such has not previously been sanctioned by the Directors.

4. Occupiers of a smaller portion of Ground than One Hundred and Fifty Square Feet, shall not be accounted as Shareholders of the Company, nor have any voice in the direction of its affairs, neither shall they have a right to enclose the Grounds they occupy, nor erect Monuments thereon.

Stockholders.

1. The Stockholders and Proprietors shall meet Annually on the first Monday in May, for the enactment of Bye Laws and the Election of Directors; in default of such Meeting, the Directors to continue in office, and the Laws in force until the next Meeting.

2. Each Proprietor of a Lot of or exceeding One Hundred and Fifty Square Feet, shall be eligible to vote, or be elected as a Director.

3. Each Stockholder shall be entitled by himself or proxy to one vote for every Share held by him, and to be elected as a Director (no Stockholder by himself or proxies having more than One Hundred votes), until the whole paid up Stock, with interest at the rate of Eight per centum per annum be paid, when the Stockholders, as such, shall cease to have any interest in the Cemetery, and the Property shall be vested in the then and future Proprietors of Lots of not less each than One Hundred and Fifty Square Feet.

Directors.

1. The Directors shall meet as often as necessary. Meetings to be called by the Secretary

at the order of the President or Three Directors. Five to form a Quorum.

2. The Directors shall appoint a Secretary and Treasurer, a Superintendent, and a Landscape Gardener.

3. The Directors shall confine their annual expenditure to their annual income.

4. The Treasurer's Accounts and Books shall be audited by a person not a Director, whose Certificate must accompany the Directors' Report to the Annual Meeting.

5. The Directors shall order sales of Lots, and by orders of the Board only, give directions to the Officers as to the management of the affairs of the Company.

6. The Directors are authorized to call for further Instalments of Stock if required, until the whole shall have been paid : should any Stockholder refuse or neglect to comply with any such call, he shall forfeit any sum he may have already paid.

7. Half the proceeds of all sales shall be laid out on the Cemetery : the other Half to be applied Half-yearly to the liquidation of the balance of purchase money, until the same be paid in full with interest : after which to be paid to the Stockholders until they be paid in full with interest at the rate of Eight per centum. The whole income to be thereafter expended on the Cemetery.

Secretary and Treasurer.

1. The Secretary shall keep a Book in which he shall minute all proceedings of the Meetings ;

which Book shall always be open to the inspection of Stockholders and Proprietors.

2. He shall keep a Book, in which he shall enter when paid or received, all monies belonging to the Company, balancing the same annually, and furnishing a balance sheet at the Annual Meeting.

3. He shall when sales of Lots are made, give a Certificate to the purchaser under the Seal of the Company, for each of which he shall receive One Dollar, keeping a Register Book, and numbering the Lots from One upwards.

4. He shall keep a Book in which he shall enter the weekly returns of Interments made by the Superintendent.

5. He shall deposit in such Bank as the Directors may order, to the credit of the Company, and to be drawn upon by the President and himself, all monies received by him over and above Ten Pounds to be retained to meet Contingencies.

Superintendent.

1. The Superintendent shall have the general management within the Cemetery, subject to the Bye Laws of the Company, and to orders from the Board.

2. He shall in laying off the Ground take directions from the Landscape Gardener.

3. He shall employ as many laborers as the Board may direct, paying them in full every Saturday, by an order on the Treasurer, stating the wages in detail.

4. He shall make sale of such produce as the ground may yield, paying over to the Treasurer the amount of such sales when made.

5. He shall not by himself, or any within his control, receive money from Visitors.

6. He shall collect Burial Fees and Fees of Interment in the Public and Poor Ground, paying over the same to the Treasurer, but shall not sell or receive the price of Lots.

7. He shall receive applications from persons wishing Lots, and lay the same before the Board.

8. He shall make a return weekly to the Secretary, of all interments made.

Visitors.

1. Visitors on Horseback must dismount and lead their horses.

2. No Vehicle shall be driven in the Cemetery at a rate faster than a walk

3. No Visitor shall gather any Flowers, nor break nor injure any Tree, Shrub or Plant in the Cemetery.

4. No Visitor shall take Firearms into the Cemetery.

5. None shall be admitted on Sundays but Proprietors with their families and friends.

6. Visitors are requested not to offer money to any person connected with the Cemetery.

7. Visitors are requested to keep on the walks and avenues, and not trespass on the borders or through the woods.

8. Visitors are prohibited from bringing in or using any refreshments within the Cemetery.

9. It shall be the duty of the Superintendent to see these Rules enforced.

ADDENDA TO BYE LAWS.

(*See page* 18.)

At a Meeting of the Directors of the Saint John Rural Cemetery Company, May 5th, A. D., 1858,

The following Resolution was carried :

Whereas, The Directors of the Rural Cemetery have found great difficulty in collecting the outstanding debts,

Therefore Resolved, That in future all Lots shall be paid for at the time of Sale ;

And further Resolved, That all Lots nominally sold, but not paid for by the purchasers, be disposed of to any applicant, unless the said Lots are paid for forthwith.

Extract from the Minutes,

EDWARD B. PETERS,
Secretary and Treasurer.

(*See page* 20.)

At the Annual General Meeting of the Shareholders and Proprietors of the Saint John Rural Cemetery Company, April 4th, A. D., 1859,

The following Resolution was carried :

Moved by Dr. Botsford seconded by Mr. J. M. Walker, "That the seventh section of the Bye Laws, under the head of Directors, be rescinded." Which is carried unanimously.

Extract from the Minutes.

EDWARD B. PETERS,
Secretary and Treasurer.

At the Annual General Meeting of the Shareholders and Proprietors of the Saint John Rural Cemetery Company, 5th May, A. D., 1851 :—

The following amendment to the Bye-Laws of the Company, was passed unanimously, viz. :

To the 1st Bye Law, under the head of

Proprietors.

after the words *erect Monuments;* insert the following, viz. :—

" thereon (except that no Slab shall be set in any other than a horizontal position.")

Extract from the Minutes.

EDWARD B. PETERS,

Secretary and Treasurer.

LIST OF PROPRIETORS OF LOTS,

In the Rural Cemetery.

1. George P. Peters.
2. Henry Gilbert.
3. Edward B. Peters.
4. Robert Jardine.
5. John M. Walker.
6. James Pettingell.
7. William G. Lawton.
8. LeBaron Botsford.
9. William Parks.
10. John M. Campbell.
11. John G. Sharp.
12. John Henderson.
13. James M'Gregor.
14. William O. Smith.
15. John D. Purdy.
16. Henry P. Sancton.
17. Richard Dalton.
18. Mrs. Sarah Millidge.
19. Robert Kedey.
20. John C. White.
21. William M'Auley.
22. James Cooper.
23. Peter Reed.
24. Commissioners of Marine Hospital.
25. William Duffy.
26. James Agnew.
27. Robert D. M'Arthur.
28. John W. Craig.
29. Christopher Noble.
30. Mrs. Ettie Wiley.
31. Mrs. Mary J. Roden.

32. John Vassie.
33. John Smith.
34. Thomas Gilchrist.
35. Alexander Gilchrist.
36. James Howe.
37. Richard Heanes.
38. Fairbanks Committee.
39. Richard Thompson.
40. Thomas L. Taylor.
41. Peter Reed.
42. John Hastings.
43. Alexander McL. Seely.
44. Alexander Grier.
45. Thomas Bissett.
46. James Dunn.
47. John Dunn.
48. Robert Mills.
49. Thomas P. Crane.
50. George A. Garrison.
51. Mrs. Eliza Gove.
52. Richard Cromley.
53. James M'Millan.
54. Henry W. Sewell.
55. Samuel Williams.
56. John Mount Thain.
57. Nathaniel Adams.
58. John Nevin.
59. Henry Henderson.
60. John Pettingell (Estate)
61. Aaron Hastings.
62. Robert Armstrong.
63. William H. Williams.
64. Sarah and James Burrell.
65. John Ferguson.
66. John F. Marsters.
67. William Gabriel.
68. James Kerr.
69. James W. Disbrow.
70. Julius L. Inches.

71. John Pollok.
72. Hiram Betts.
73. Nathan S. DeMill.
74. Mrs. Mary Ann Bell.
75. Thomas Reed.
76. Adam Jack.
77. Mark Varley (Estate.)
78.   Collins.
79. Joseph Read.
80. John Walker.
81. William Warn.
82. Ebenezer M'Nichol.
83. James Capston.
84. Thomas C. Everitt.
85. Daniel J. M'Laughlin.
86. Charles M'Lauchlan.
87. James D. Lewin.
88. Rev. William Donald.
89. James M'Lean.
90. Alonzo A. Darrow.
91. Thomas Smith.
92. James W. Peters.
93. Thomas M'Henry.
94.   Milligan.
95. William Botsford.
96. John Hay.
97. Archibald Fraser.
98. David Johnston.
99. William H. Bowyer.
100. Alexander Anderson.
101. Charles B. Simpson (Estate)
102. James Reed.
103. Thomas W. Daniel.
104.   Lordly.
105. Mrs. F. A. Drury.
106. Charles Drury.
107. Robert L. Hazen.
108. Charles Hazen.
109. William Hazen (Estate).

110. Ward Chipman.
111. Robert F. Hazen.
112. Andrew Reed.
113. Robert Finley.
114. William Finley.
115. George F. Robertson.
116. Samuel Ramsay.
117. Frederick G. Harrison.
118. George W. Roberts.
119. George W. Roberts.
120. Robert Middlemore.
121. Thomas Proud.
122. R. W. Crookshank, Jun.
123. David Reid.
124. Henry Nicholls.
125. John Kennedy.
126. Benjamin C. Chaloner.
127. Archibald Cook.
128. Thomas Gass.
129. Alexander Campbell.
130. Joseph H. D. Colwell.
131. William D. W. Hubbard.
132. Justices of Peace, Saint John.
133. Mrs. Mary Craig.
134. John Haws, Jun.
135. Mrs. Elizabeth Clarihue.
136. John A. Morrison.
137. Samuel Taylor.
138. Robert Reed.
139. James H. Hegan.
140. Thomas Parks.
141. James Smith.
142. John Hegan.
143. John Brown.
144. James Keohan.
145. Henry Austin.
146. Edward DeWolf.
147. Richard P. M'Givern.
148. George Priestly.

149. John W. J. Beard.
150. Mrs. Mary Leavitt.
151. Robert Nesbitt.
152. Archibald T. Heney.
153. Andrew Hennigar.
154. Andrew Gilmour.
155. Mrs. Maria Busby.
156. James H. Dorman.
157. Thomas R. Gordon.
158. Ross Selfridge.
159. Charles Brown.
160. John J. Akerley.
161. James J. Christie.
162. William Jack.
163. Charles C. Petch.
164. Mrs. Jane Paul.
165. David Boddie.
166. William Bookhout.
167. Moses Lawrence.
168. Alexander Yeats.
169.   Halcrow.
170. Trustees McKay's Church.
171. Thomas T. Hanford.
172. George Scoullar.
173. John H. Robilliard.
174.
175. John Moore.
176. William H. Owen.
177. George Wassaon.
178. John Budge.
179.
180. John Hammond.
181. William H. Brown.
182. William Thomson.
183. David Tapley.
184. Daniel Hatfield.
185. Christopher Smiler, Jun.
186. Mrs. Ann Nevins.
187. Samuel B. Estey.

188. Charles L. Street.
189. Isaac Woodward.
190. David Seelye.
191. William H. Patterson.
192. William Peters.
193. Archibald Brown.
194. Dr. James Ruddick.
195. Thomas Plummer.
196. Mrs. Mary Humbert.
197. Stephen E. Gerow.
198. William N. Venning.
199. William H. Keltic.
200. James Stewart.
201. Ewen Cameron.
202. James Macfarlane.
203. Robert Thomson.
204. William Brundage.
205. James S. Harris.
206. William Cockran.
207. Duncan Brown.
208. Henry Robertson.
209. James H. Venning.
210.
211.
212. Thomas Miller.
213. William White.
214. Joseph Smith.
215. William Steven.
216. Richard Seely.
217. Noah Disbrow, Sen.
218. Thomas W. Henery.
219. George S. DeForest.
220. Rev. William Ferrie.
221.   Jarvis.
222. John Marvin.
223. Allan K. Dalling.
224.   Hunter.
225. John Wisdom.
226. Andrew Mulhollen.

227. Stephen K. Brundage.
228. David M'Cullough.
229. Robert Nixon.
230. William Dunham.
231. Mrs. Ellinor Gerow.
232. Thomas Sandall.
233. Thomas W. Peters.
234. Bartlett Lingley.
235. Mrs. Isabell E. Wishart.
236.
237. Samuel Neill.
238.
239.
240. George Morrisey.
241. James Logan.
242. George J. Pine.
243. John Sime.
244. Andrew Wilson.
245. Henry Fotherby.
246. James Slocomb.
247. Mrs. Eliza W. Very.
248. Robert Hunter.
249. Elijah Barker.
250. George H. Laskey.
251. Augustus Quick.
252. John Lean.
253. Mrs. Jane Johnston.
254.   Rennick.
255. Edmund Kaye.
256. James J. Kaye.
257. Robert Polley.
258. Samuel L. Tilley.
259. John Armstrong.
260. John Cox.
261. Charles Humphreys.
262. John C. M'Intosh.
263. James M'Nicholl.
264. Bart. Nesbitt.
265. Charles Thompson.

266. George F. Thompson.
267. James Sullivan.
268. Gabriel Fowler.
269. William Rodgers.
270. William M'Aulcy.
271. John Anderson.
272. Henry Leavitt.
273. John Smith.
274. Edward Whittaker.
275. John Murray.
276. William Leonard.
277.   Nixon.
278. William Henderson.
279.   M'Donald.
280.   Cormack.
281. John B. Johnson.
282. Hugh Chisholm.
283. John Turnbull.
284. Samuel Davison.
285 Mrs, Mary Bairdain.
286.
287. Robert Hume.
288. John Kain.
289. Thomas Main.
290. James Hardy.
291. Alexander Sime.
292. Henry Graham.
293.   M'Auley.
294. Thomas C. Humbert.
295.   Cody.
296. Thomas Gardiner.
297.   Sullivan.
298. Archibald Gillies.
299. Samuel Crawford.
300. James Logan.
301. James H. Fairweather.
302. George N. Smith.
303. James M. Decker.
304. Francis Ferguson.

305. Douglas B. Stevens.
306. Henry Chubb.
307. James H. Akerley.
308. Andrew R. Wetmore.
309. William Hayward.
310. John Smith.
311. William Bryden.
312. Edward J. Brass.
313. Mrs. Martha M. Smiler.
314. George Peebles.
315. James W. Rupert.
316. John Walker.
317. John W. Gray.
318. Duncan Brown.
319. Thomas Harding.
320. Mrs. Jane Welsh
321. Mrs. Frances Gimber.
322. George Eaton.
323. James H. Haddon.
324. Hester E. Knollin.
325. William W. Emslie.
326. William Fisher.
327. James Hutchison.
328. Mary A. Canby.
329. James Green.
330. Henry Hennigar.
331. Archibald M'Vicar.
332. Robert Kedey.
333. Thomas Lamb.
334. John Rowling.
335. Magnus Spence.
336. Joseph Stephenson.
337. Joseph Irvin.
338. John Corbit.
339. Jeremiah Gove.
340.
341. Mary Crawford.
342. Thomas Beveridge.
343. James Blair.

**

344. William Causey.
345. William Davidson.
346. James Barber.
347. William Dudne.
348. Samuel Davis.
349. William Ellison.
350.
351. Andrew Crawford
352. John Day.
353. William Brown.
354. Samuel Bancroft.
355. William Pardoe.
356. Mrs. Susanna Carr
357. Robert Carr.
358. Richard S. Dickson.
359. Samuel Dalzell.
360. William Breeze.
361. Mrs. Jane Purdy.
362. John Flewwelling.
363. Gilford Flewwelling.
364. Joel Reading.
365. Edward W. Greenwood.
366. Oliver Bailey.
367. Thomas Clerke.
368. Samuel Gardiner.
369. John Humbert.
370. Edna Kelly.
371. Ebenezer Stephen.
372. George Cathers.
373. John W. Cudlip.
374. Edwin Fisher.
375. Robert F. Smith.
376. Mrs. Mary McCutcheon.
377.
378. John Logan.
379. Robert Collins.
380. John McNeill.
381. John Scott.
382. Robert Hannah.
383.   Murray.

384. Samuel P. Osgood.
385.
386. Henry Marshall.
387. Mrs. Jane Hood.
388. Peter Sinclair.
389.
390. Mrs. Jane McKelvey
391. Samuel Garrett.
392. Thomas Kelly.
393. John Marshall.
394. David Miller.
395. John Heustin.
396. William Small.
397. William Hutchinson.
398.   McLardy.
399.   Norris.
400. George Quinn.
401. Margaret Magee.
402. David J. Schureman.
403. John Rolston.
404. Alexander C. O. Trentowsky.
405. William H. Tyson.
406. Robert Mahony.
407. Francis Mahony.
408. Robert Stewart.
409. Elizabeth Smith.
410. James McCawley.
411. Robert McMurray.
412. William Rannic.
413. John Vaughan.
414. Sylvanus Whitney.
415. George N. Robinson.
416. Alexander Wark.
417. William Young.
418.   Wallis.
419. John Wilson.
420. Donald Gunn.
421. Robert Godfrey, Jr.
422. Edward T. Knowles.

423. Richard W. Thorne.
424. George Salter.
425. James N. C. Black.
426. Josiah W. Smith.
427. Adam McAffee.
428. Robert Melrose.
429. Thomas A. Paddock.
430 Samuel Allison.
431. Jacob Kay.
432. George P. Sancton.
433. Henry Dalton.
434. George Martin.
435.   Gregg.
436. William Turner.
437. John Maxwell.
438. Charles A. Hartt.
439. Joshua Bunting.
440. Hugh Clements.
441. Robert Ruddick.
442. John Sharp.
443. Otis Small.
444. Hartwell B. Crosby.
445. Edward C. Freeze.
446. John K. Keefe.
447. Ann Clarke.
448. Mary Adams.
449. Henry Delue.
450. Charles E. Potter.
451. James Madden.
452. Robert Sheraton.
453. George Flemming.
454. Charles J. Waterberry.
455. James McLean.
456. Frank Giles.
457. John Robertson.
458. Arthur McLean.
459. Charles Knox.
460. John Herrington.
461. William G. Herrington.

462. Edward E. Lockhart.
463. William Stirling.
464. Thomas Armstrong.
465. Jonathan Anderson.
466. Frederick C. Frith.
467. William Courtney.
468. Andrew Brown.
469. John Totten.
470. Hastings & Armstrong.
471. Thomas Dale.
472. Daniel Haslam.
473. James Kenney.
474. Aaron Hastings.
475. Robert Armstrong
476. William Hewitt.
477. Henry M. Ladd.
478. James Aiton.
479. George Suffrin.
480. Carson Flood.
481. Charles H. Tucker.
482. William W. Turnbull.
483. Charles T. Dickson.
484. Alexander Rankine,
485. William Anderson, Sen.
486. William Shives.
487. James Leetch.
488. Levi H. Waterhouse.
489. Charles W. Barteaux.
490. Charles H. Fairweather.
491. William McCullam.
492. Henry W. Purdy.
493. Thomas McCormack.
494. Archibald Rowan.
495. John Melick (Estate.)
496. George D. Godsoe.
497.   White.
498. Frederick W. Wood.
499. Gilbert Murdock.
500.   Haws.

501. Israel S. Lawson.
502. Peter Y. Malcolmson.
503. John S. Richey.
504. John Haws, senr.
505. Mrs.   Hunter.
506.   Sullivan.
507.
508.
509.
510.
511. Stephen Howard.
512. Robert Graham.
513. Robert Laskey.
514. William Parks, Jun.
515. Asa D. Blakslee.
516. John Fisher.
517.   Smith.
518. Henry Akerley.
519. William Cameron.
520. Alexander Christie.
521. Charles N. Perkins.
522. Ross Woodrow.
523. William H. Smith.
524. Myles B. Smith.
525. William T. Pratt.
526. Ann Heanes.
527. John T. Stanton.
528. William Ritchie.
529. Richard G. Hall.
530. John Jenkins.
531. Archibald Page.
532. William Bayard.
533. Frederick A. Wiggins.
534. George Kee.
535. James Elsdon.
536. Mrs. Ann Cassidy.
537. Aaron Armstrong.
538. Alexander Wilson.
539. David V. Roberts.

540. Jonathan Cassidy.
541. Alexander Torry.
542. Charles H. Estabrooks.
543. Margaret Hutchings.
544. William H. Harrison.
545. Henry Osborne.
546. William H. Knodell.
547. John McIntyre.
548. James Horsfall.
549. William Livingston.
550.   Leary.
551. Mrs. Hannah Ball.
552. David Cronk.
553. George Hutchinson.
554. Thomas Logan.
555. George W. Smith.
556. Robert Keltie.
557. Thomas Rankine.
558. Joseph Armstrong.
559. Alexander McKenzie.
560. Solomon Hersey.
561. John Brown.
562. Mrs. Susan McLean.
563. James J. Fellows.
564. Joseph E. N. Holder.
565. Joseph Jenkins.
566. Samuel Holman.
567.   Simpson.
568. Mrs Jane Grant.
569. Robertson Bayard.
570. Edwin Hooper.
571. John Fitzpatrick.
572. John Latimour.
573. William Boyne.
574. Archibald McLean.
575. Mrs. Albenia S. Boyd.
576. John Kennedy.
577. Joseph Johnston.
578. John McFate.

579. Mrs. Louisa Hunter.
580. William Till.
581. Thomas Renton.
582. Robert R. Sneden.
583.   Graham.
584.   Thomas.
585. Corey O'Dell.
586. Zebedee G. Gable.
587. David J. Merritt.
588. Robert J. Alexander.
589. Mrs. Harriet Clerke.
590. John McGregor.
591. Thomas McKenzie.
592.   Lewis.
593.   Irvin.
594. John Cowan.
595. William Thompson.
596. Mrs. Lucy Ann Sutherland.
597. Samuel Parks.
598. Thomas E. G. Tisdale.
599.
600. David Magee.
601. John J. Hogan.
602. John W. Nicholson.
603. Charles Wilson.
604. John McMoran.
605. Isabella Doak.
606. John Fraser.
607.   Estey.
608. George R. Price.
609. William Allingham.
610. David Dunham.
611. George C. Dunham.
612. Mrs. Mary Ferguson.
613. James McAlary.
614. James A. Whitney.
615. Joshua Belyea.
616. James Bennett.
617.   Milligan.

618. Mathias Hamm.
619.
620. Lewis Waters.
621.   Jamieson.
622. Thomas F. Raymond.
623.   Saneton.
624. Daniel J. Seely.
625. Jeremiah Thompson.
626. Thomas S. Estey.
627. John Storms.
628. Frederick James.
629. Stephen Blizard.
630. John Johnston.
631.   Mahony.
632. George Plumpton.
633. Sarah V. Hunter.
634. Joshua S. Turner.
635.   Crookshank.
636. Michael Thompson.
637. George King.
638. Mark N. Powers.
639. Alexander Robertson.
640. John Sears.
641. William Dunlop.
642. George E. Snyder.
643. William C. Godsoe.
644. Thomas A. Godsoe.
645. Robert Scott.
646. Samuel Watson.
647. Zachariah B. Roberts.
648. William Turner.
649. Harriet and Caroline Vieth.
650.   Sulis.
651. Edward Rubens.
652. James Stockford.
653. Robert Gilbraith.
654. Robert Whetsel.
655. George Lane.
656. Elisha and J. Willard Broad.

657. William Short.
658. Charlotte Neil.
659. David Buckley.
660. John H. Foster.
661. James G. Melick.
662. Marri A. Cuming.
663.   Cutler.
664. John Duncan.
665. George Smith.
666. James E. Barnes.
667. Joseph Pritchard.
668.
669. William McNeill.
670. Gilbert T. Ray.
671. James Dyall.
672. William Wallace.
673. Mrs. Mary Paddock.
674. John E. Turnbull.
675. Joseph G. Whitley.
676. Elisha Sibley.
677. David Munro.
678. Thomas Hatheway.
679. James R. McLean.
680. James Hamilton.
681. Richard Calvert.
682. Miss Ann Thompson.
683.   Brundage.
684. Thomas Crozier.
685. James Brayley.
686. John Lynam.
687.   Jordan.
688. George Philps.
689. Jonas Howe.
690. Henry Mahony.
691.   Perkins.
692. Robert Stewart.
693. Roderick Ross.
694.   Norris.
695. Benjamin Hevenor.

696. William Ackerley.
697. Mrs. Elizabeth Taylor.
698. John J. Munroe.
699. Robert G. Moran.
700. Mrs. Ann McAuley.
701. James Marshall.
702. George and John D. Short.
703. Jacob D. Underhill.
704. James Beatty.
705. Peter Cormack.
706. William Lunn.
707. John Simpson.
708. William Goodman.
709. Mrs. Margaret McKee.
710.   Porteous.
711. Thomas M. Smith.
712. Stephen Wiggins.
713. Robert Cruikshank.
714.   Hall.
715. Thomas A. Barker.
716. Henry Vaughan.
717. William Gorman.
718. Eliza Rawleigh.
719. Ann Hall.
720. Eliza Barlow.
721. Ezekiel McLeod.
722. William and James Ferguson
723. John McCulloch.
724. Humphrey Peel.
725. Edward Allison.
726. John Kirk.
722. Robert Stubs.